DECORATING THE T

LOOK WHO'S COMING TO TOWN

2

ELFIE SELFIE

Only two of the close-ups below are in the main picture.
Can you find them?

A

B

C

D

TREE TRAIN

WARM PASTRIES! HOT CHOCOLATE!

COCOA AND COOKIES

SPECIAL DELIVERY

WINTER WONDERLAAAAAAND!

YUMMY RIDE

Find and count all the pretzels hidden on the carousel.

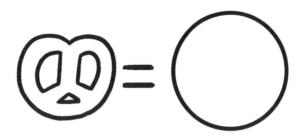

SNOWBALL FIGHT!

AN ELF'S WORK IS NEVER DONE

NEEDS MORE APPLES

NO, DEFINITELY MORE CARROTS!

DEAR SANTA ...

Can you spot the eight differences between
these two pictures?

PRESENTS FOR PUPS

CAT COMES DOWN, STAR GOES UP

THE SWEETEST HOLIDAY

Help the baker organize these pastries so there is only one of each kind in every column and row.

WAITING FOR THE SNOW BUS

ALL ABOARD

BUS 318

JH-0049

WHEEEEEE!

WAKEY WAKEY!

WHERE DID I PARK?

Help Santa find his way to his sleigh.

START

FINISH

FESTIVE FUN AND GAMES

SNACK BREAK

LOOKING FOR SANTA

HO HO HO!

CAN WE LIVE HERE?

TINSEL TANGLE

Follow the lines to find out which house Santa
is going to visit next.

WHO'S COMING DOWN THE CHIMNEY?

RACING THROUGH THE SNOW

FINISHING TOUCH

HAS SANTA BEEN YET?

PRESENT PAIRS

Which of these presents is not part of a matching pair?

JINGLE ALL THE WAY

SWEET AND COSY

THANKS, SANTA!

Connect the dots to see what the girl got for Christmas.

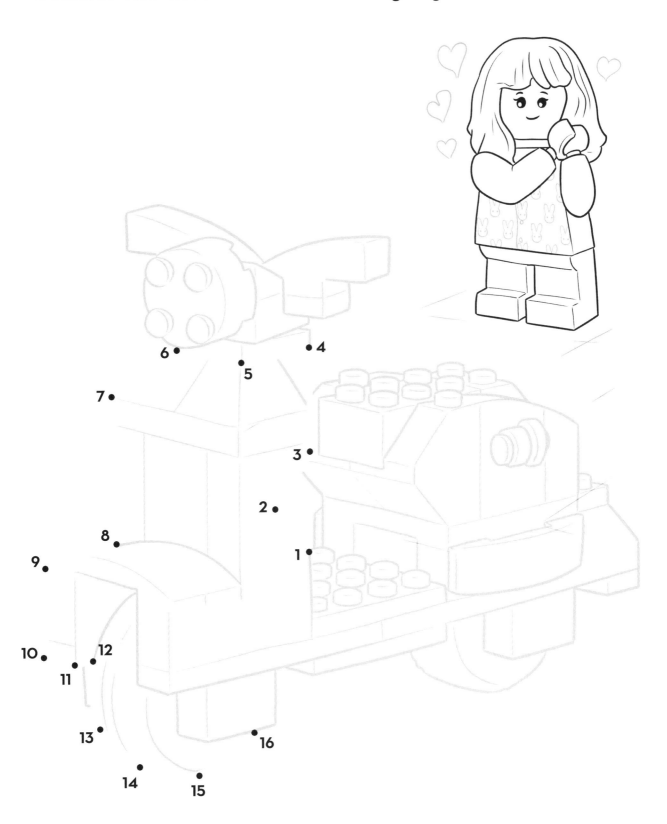

HERE'S TO CHRISTMAS!

PARTY TIME

SEE YOU NEXT CHRISTMAS!

ANSWERS

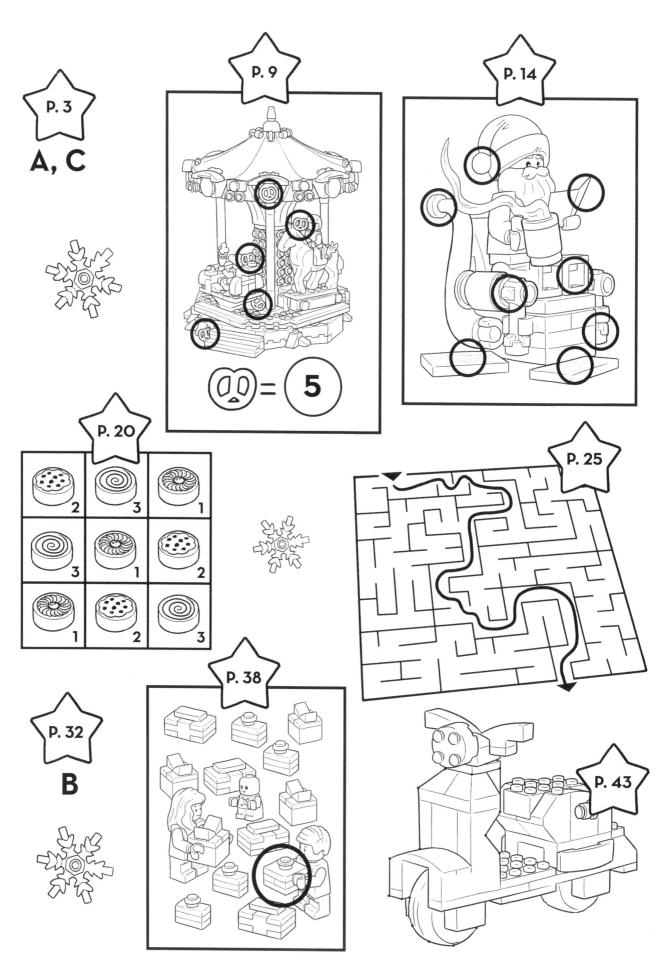